A Bedtime Story

Jason Luke

Copyright © 2016 Jason Luke

Let's talk about sex, you and I.

Or, more accurately, let's talk about sex and seduction.

I mean that's why you invited me into your home, after all, isn't it?

Apparently I'm a guy who has some kind of a reputation for telling erotic stories that engage the senses and imagination, and right now you're in the mood to listen to me. So let's have the conversation – just you and me. We'll spend an intimate evening together, alone in our own little world where only you and I exist for the next few hours. We'll talk about sex, intimacy, erotica, and all those things that go together to create a sense of arousal.

And we'll be honest with each other.

You see the attraction here is mutual. You've invited me into your home because you want to be aroused, but I've come here because you fascinate me.

I mean that.

I want to know what you think and how you feel. I want to watch your face while I talk, and read the subtle changes of your expression. I want to see the way your eyes change when I share my stories and remember where your breathing quickens.

I want to know you, and what turns you on.

It's important to me – very important – because the art of seducing a woman is all about being able to read the signs… and as a writer of erotica, I need to know women in order to touch them, inspire them, and stimulate them.

Will you help me?

I'll tell you my stories and all you need to do is relax and listen. I know you don't *need* to hear what I have to say… I'm the one who *needs* to talk, because I have a lot of stories to share, and I feel I can talk to you. We have that type of connection – the kind of relationship that's personal, but not so intimate that it will ever become awkward. I can talk to you, and you can be yourself. That's how this works.

But do me a favor first. I want you to find a quiet place alone, somewhere you really can relax and tune out the world. I want your attention, and I want you to be comfortable.

Maybe it's that big chair in your living room, with the lights dimmed down low and the drapes drawn. Or maybe it's behind the closed door of your bedroom where no one can interrupt us. We'll need to be alone for this. I have you for a few hours and I don't want anything to interrupt us.

Now take your panties off.

Go on – it's okay. In fact it's perfectly fine.

It's what I want you to do.

You see these stories I have to tell you are *those* kind of stories – they're erotic memories I want to share with you because I need to work out some things in my head, and talking about them helps. I hope listening to them is arousing for you. As I said a few minutes ago, that's why I'm here with you right now, isn't it? You invited me into your home because you're in the mood to be aroused, and I have some stories I want to share.

So take off your panties and get comfortable. Very comfortable.

Good girl.

I want to talk to you about erotica, and I want you to feel free to touch yourself. Tonight I would like for you to feel completely uninhibited – maybe even a little reckless. Remember how you used to be before life and all its responsibilities started beating you down, stealing your time? Well this is our special time together, and I want you to shut out the rest of life's madness and spend the evening with me.

Just me.

Connecting intimately.

Glide your fingers gently over your body for me. Don't rush. Take your time. Make it one of those casual caresses where your touch lingers deliciously. You can imagine they're my hands if you like, or maybe the hands of a lover, boyfriend or husband. The main thing is to set the mood between us and to establish the bond of understanding we have. If I'm going to be honest and share my stories with you, then I need you to be honest with me in your reactions.

Feel free to touch yourself if the stories arouse you. No one is in the room apart from you and me – and I won't tell. In fact, it would be nice to watch you. It would be arousing to see you with your eyes closed, listening to my stories while your fingers caress your body and to hear those soft seductive sounds you make when you're turned on.

Let yourself go. I know this might not be normal, but neither is this conversation we're having, right? Shed your reserve, let go of any inhibitions. This evening will only work for both of us if you surrender yourself to your feelings and emotions – the sensual ones. Let yourself be taken away and forget about feeling awkward. I don't want to see the woman you show the rest of the world. I want to see the real you – that private erotic piece of your soul that you keep secret. Show me that woman tonight – the real you. Let your hair down and be yourself.

Really. Take a deep breath and let it all go.

I want to spend an hour or two alone with you, in the intimate darkness, and I want you to be a woman. That's what you want too, right? You want to feel like you're a woman for a few hours – not a mom, not a sister or a wife. You want something secret and sexy that is yours alone – a private fantasy place you can escape to in your mind where the rest of the world falls away and it's just you and me, talking.

I'm not going to raise my voice. This isn't some kind of theatre performance that relies on stage effects or lighting.

This is raw and it's real.

And it's intimate. Just you. And me.

Tonight I'll whisper to you, I'll talk like it's just you and me alone together speaking in the hushed tones that lovers do, if you like. And I'll be patient. I'm in no hurry. I'm grateful for the time you can give me, and I *want* to spend this time alone with you. Together, we can pass a few pleasant hours in each other's company and no one need ever know that I was here with you now. I won't tell anyone. Will you?

No. Tonight it's just you and me, alone, together in your special place with the lights down low and the world left far, far behind.

It's like a sexy date; an erotic encounter at a secret location that only you and I know about.

Are you relaxed?

Are you comfortable?

As soon as you're ready, we can begin.

* * *

I lived the lifestyle of a Master for quite a few years when I was in a long-term relationship with a woman I met in my mid-thirties. Her name was Steffie and she was a tall, slim, dark haired woman who had the body and moves of a dancer.

Sometimes, I still think about her at night. On occasions, when I cannot sleep, Steffie comes to me during that time just before I dream, and the memories of her are always the same.

Does that happen to you − or is it just me? Is there someone from your past who comes to you in the quiet, lonely moments? Someone who makes you smile when you think of them, or someone you turn to when you're mind slips into your private fantasies?

Yes, fantasy.

Every woman has a fantasy.

Some of the women I have known have been wildly imaginative – eager and willing sexual partners where the relationship was more physical than emotional. Others... well there have been plenty of them too, but they're not the ladies I think of late at night – and they're not the ladies I want to talk to you about, nor, I suspect the ladies you would want to hear about.

No, the ladies I want to share stories about are the ones who have left a profound impression on me – those women whose memories are branded into my mind because of their willingness to be adventurous, erotic *women*.

But before we go further, I forgot to ask you something, and this is a conversation after all. I know I'm here to entertain and arouse you this evening, but a healthy relationship requires give and take, right?

So tell me – do *you* have a fantasy?

You don't have to tell me what it is – perhaps we aren't close enough yet for you to feel comfortable sharing the details – but can you at least acknowledge that you do have a fantasy?

Just nod your head.

Good girl.

Thank you.

A lot of ladies I write for have fantasies about the **BDSM** lifestyle. The images in their mind are very powerful, their fantasies dramatic and intense. I get that. Having lived the lifestyle as a Master for some time, I know for a fact that the interplay between a Dom and his submissive can be charged with a sexual energy that is difficult to duplicate. The interplay of roles can be highly seductive – intoxicating.

Addictive.

Have you ever fantasized about being sexually and emotionally submissive to a strong man who knows what he wants and gets what he goes after, without ever compromising his integrity or the safety of the woman who has placed herself in his charge?

Have you ever dreamed about what it would be like to *really* experience just a couple of erotic-filled hours at the command of such a man?

How would you feel? Does the idea excite you?

Have you ever wanted to say *'yes, Sir!'* to a man?

Try it, now. I promise it's okay. No one will ever know. Just whisper the words for me.

Say, 'yes, Sir!'

Good girl.

I'd love to watch you on your knees, with your hands clasped behind you, your back arched just a little, and your hips thrust forward... your lips slightly parted, your eyes like dark pools of desire...

I really would.

That's okay, isn't it?

It's okay that I fantasize about you – after all, you're the reason I'm here – the enigma of you; the mystery that I can't quite solve. That's who you are to me.

You're the only one I'm being intimate with tonight; the only one I'm sharing this moment with.

I'd like to watch you from the dark corners of your room and hear your breathing become a little hectic. It will be our secret – our sexy secret. You see I really want to watch you pleasure yourself. I want my stories to arouse you – to make you feel uninhibited and crazy turned on. That's the *real reason* I'm with you tonight.

I want you to cum for me before I leave.

Sorry. I seem to be wandering away from the story I was telling you about my life as a Master with Steffie, but I will get back to it. I mean there's plenty of time, right? We've just begun our night together and I said I wouldn't rush. I said I would be patient because I want you to enjoy these few hours and I want it to be an unforgettable experience for you. There's just one last thing...

Are you okay with some graphic language?

I'm no great author. I'm just a guy trying to tell you a story, trying to whisper words and paint images in your mind that you will find stimulating. For my entire career I've wrestled to find the right word – the one that captures the essence of what I am trying to express. Sometimes I get it right. Most of the time I fail. But I don't use graphic language for shock value, so I hope you'll be understanding tonight. I feel like I can be honest with you. I feel like we have some special chemistry happening here, and if I'm going to tell you my stories, then sometimes I'm going to have to use words that only belong in erotica novels.

You're okay with that, aren't you?

They're not the kind of words I would use if I met you on the street, but we're way past that point now, aren't we. Look around. I'm here with you in your home because you invited me in, and we're alone, you and I. We're in the soft seductive darkness of your special place and I'm watching you from the corner of my eye, gazing at you with a look somewhere between wonder and fascination. I want to know the dark sexy secrets that lurk behind your eyes, but for now that can wait. Because I've come to entertain you, and that means I first need to share with you my story about Steffie.

Share?

Yes. Because I want you to feel involved in these tales I tell you. I want you to feel what the ladies in my stories felt, and be able to imagine yourself in their place. I want this to be something intimate we share. After tonight our relationship will never be quite the same.

Now, spread your legs for me... just let your knees fall gently open because I want you to be completely relaxed.

Steffie was into the BDSM lifestyle, and maybe that's why I'm sharing her story with you. When I met her she was like a beautiful flower deprived of sunlight – she had lost herself in a series of short meaningless relationships and forgot that secret part of her that was aroused – that erotic flame that flickered because she had tried to be every man's fantasy instead of living the fantasy that compelled her – that made her complete.

Maybe you can relate, right? Maybe you're nodding your head right now. I can't see you in the shadows, but I sense some sympathetic understanding for Steffie's plight. I guess a lot of ladies lose themselves by trying too hard to be what someone else wants them to be.

The first time I told Steffie to touch herself she was laying on my bed with her legs spread, and a blindfold tied tight across her eyes. It was a warm summer's afternoon and the windows were open. A gentle breeze came drifting off the ocean and I could smell the salt in the air.

Steffie was lying with her hands clenched into anxious little fists beside her. Her legs were wide apart and she was wearing white lingerie; stockings that ended above her knees and then a corset cinched tight so that it lifted her breasts and her nipples peaked like hard little berries above the lace trim of the cups. White lace suspender ribbons connected the top of the stockings to the bottom of the lingerie.

She wore no panties – but Steffie never wore panties.

It was a rule of mine.

I think the blindfold made those early submissive sessions we shared easier for her. The darkness – the sense of detachment seemed to make it easier for her to react and respond to my commands. It was like a thin veil between us that freed her to be pliant and responsive. I guess it's a little like our situation right now – the place you and I find ourselves. We're alone together, but that shroud of darkness between where you are and where I'm standing watching and talking to you... it's a comfort maybe – just enough anonymity for you to feel comfortable touching yourself, trailing your fingers over the soft creamy flesh of your inner thigh...

The darkness gives us all that freedom, don't you think?

Steffie was lying with her lips moist and parted, frowning just a little to get a sense of where I was, what I was doing. I prowled around the bed for a long time, drinking in the erotic fantasy of her; she was quivering with that rare kind of sexual anticipation that seemed to heighten all her senses, made her skin come alive to my every touch. I leaned over the bed and trailed a line of wet kisses down the soft exposed flesh of her throat and drew one of her nipples between my teeth.

Steffie gasped – a sigh of pent up breath that turned into a groan.

"Touch yourself," I told her. *"I want to watch you pleasure yourself. I want to know what arouses you. Show me."*

For an instant she hesitated, and then one of her hands came tentatively from her side, across the flat taut muscles of her abdomen and dipped deliciously between the folds of her pussy.

It was an erotic moment I will never forget. The air seemed to crackle with sensual energy. For all it's simplicity, the act of Steffie slowly sliding one of her fingers between the glistening folds of her sex was something that stays clearly with me to this day.

I watched, mesmerized – not the actual way she moved her fingers, but rather the way her body responded. That was what intrigued me. That was what held me utterly mesmerized. It began with her breathing – the sudden tightness of each inhalation as her fingers became slick with the rising heat of her desire, and then brushed, light as butterfly wings, across the jutting button of her clit. The breath seized in her throat and her mouth fell open into a long throaty moan. I watched her face, and even behind the blindfold I sensed her eyes were screwed tightly shut.

"Keep touching yourself," I insisted. The sound of my own voice in my ears was suddenly thick with my own need. *"Make yourself cum for me."*

Steffie trapped her bottom lip between her teeth and her head turned to the side as if she had drawn all the air from around her. A rising bloom of color rose up across her chest like a blush and then her knees bent and raised, and her hips began to undulate, lifting off the bed in a slow erotic private dance.

I brushed the tips of my fingers over the lace of her corset and then the palm of my hand finally reached the exposed tanned flesh of her thigh. Steffie flinched as though the sensitive skin had been electrocuted, and the flurried touch of her fingers became more frantic – more primal... as though she had given herself over to raw instincts as old as time itself. Reason and inhibition slipped away. Steffie's breathing became hoarse explosive gasps. Her whole body began to writhe and the air in the bedroom became scented by the musky natural aroma of her excitement.

When Steffie came at last, it was with two of her own finger thrust deep inside herself while her other hand plucked at one of her nipples. She came hard, in three distinctive gasps of breath, each one torn from her throat as the grip of her orgasm clenched and then reluctantly released, washing over her like waves on a beach, exhausted and spent, drawn back into the dark depths of the ocean with the beach washed clean.

"Taste," I told her.

Without hesitating, Steffie drew her fingers to her mouth and painted the wetness of herself across her lips like glossy lipstick. She sucked her finger clean and went limp on the tangled sheets, her skin glistening with the sheen of her perspiration, her hair damp at her brow.

I told her she was beautiful and then cupped my hand over the mound of her pussy. Steffie groaned because she knew what would come next. What I was about to take from her.

Should I go on? Should I keep telling you about Steffie and that afternoon we spent together?

I feel like I'm neglecting you, and I don't want that to happen. In fact, I want you to be aroused in the same way that Steffie was.

Would you touch yourself for me now?

Do you want to?

Do it for me.

I want to watch you, just like I watched Steffie on my bed.

I really do.

I need you to feel what she felt, experience the exact same sensations of intimate privacy, sharing the moment with someone who wants only to sense the joy of your pleasure.

Intimacy and seduction.

In the meantime I will sit here in silence for a few moments and watch your face, see your mouth fall open in a tiny breathless gasp as your fingers brush across the secret heat of your pussy.

I won't say a word. I won't interrupt.

Be a good girl for me…touch yourself while I watch – and then we can continue.

* * *

Arrogance isn't arousing – it's confronting. It's crude. It substitutes the *connection* between a man and a woman – a Master and a submissive – and replaces intimacy with conceit. A man with an arrogant attitude towards women and their sexuality won't make it as a Master... and won't keep a submissive's trust and loyalty for long.

Why?

Because in missing the essential emotional connection required for a healthy BDSM relationship, an arrogant Master usually thinks a submissive is a replaceable accessory to his will.

Does that make sense?

Put yourself in the shoes of a submissive who serves an arrogant man who is interested only in his own pleasure, his own satisfaction. Imagine shrinking away from your own desires and needs just when you want more than anything else to explore your sexuality and discover those aspects of the lifestyle that deeply resonate with you.

An arrogant Master thinks a submissive can be substituted – and if they can, then it was never a healthy relationship.

Sorry. That wasn't intended to be a rant, because I didn't come here to lecture. I came here to tell you my intimate stories and to seduce you.

Forgive me.

I was just watching you from over here in the shadows, mesmerized by the way your eyebrows move and that erotic little thing your mouth does while you were touching yourself, and my mind drifted back to Steffie.

I was thinking about how we came together, and the terrible time she had searching for a man she could trust.

When we found each other, it was like fuel and fire – explosive.

That summer's afternoon in my bedroom was the catalyst for the entire relationship that followed. Maybe that's why I think of her so often at night – and why I can recall in such vivid detail each moment and every shared sensation as my hand that was cupped over her pussy began to gently massage, and Steffie began to grind herself against my palm.

I was hard – turned on by how easily Steffie had shed her inhibitions and was responding to my instructions and touch. Without instruction she rolled over on the bed and came up onto her hands and knees. I slid the blindfold from her eyes. Her bottom was the shape of a perfect love heart, the lace of the suspenders stretched tight over her flawless flesh. I flicked the retaining clips open between my thumb and forefinger and my breath came out as a low hungry growl. Steffie glanced over her shoulder at me, her eyes solemn and enigmatic. She drew the pink tip of her tongue across her lips and then lowered her head until it was propped on a pillow. She arched her back and her knees came wide apart. I dropped to my haunches behind her and slowly – deliciously – drew my tongue up along the silken folds of her pussy. Steffie gasped and then clenched her body rigid. The taste of her on my tongue was warm like honey. I licked her again and again until she began to rock her hips and sway her body back to meet my touch.

Which was exactly when I stopped, rose to my feet, and then ran my hand, stiff as a paddle, across a cheek of her bottom. Steffie knew instinctively what was about to happen, and understood why I was punishing her.

She said she was sorry. She asked me to forgive her, making her eyes huge and tragic.

"Keep count," I said ominously. *"You should know better. I touch you how and when I want. It's not for you to decide. You don't set the agenda – you respond."*

I paddled her bottom with my hand until each cheek was burning bright red, and the crimson imprint of my fingers blazed across the pale skin.

By the eighth spank, Steffie wasn't flinching any more, she was moaning softly into the pillow, stifling the raw sounds in the back of her throat and muffling her voice as she called out each slap. By the last stroke I was rubbing my hand tenderly across her flesh, salving the skin with caresses that had dipped between the juncture of her thighs and flicking my fingers across the pouting soft lips of her sex. The punishment had transformed into something deeply sensual and the wetness of her was an irresistible tease. I went to the window and drew the drapes, then stepped out of my jeans.

My cock felt as hard and hot as an iron bar drawn from the fires of a furnace. Steffie suddenly tensed. She lifted her face from the pillows and turned her head. Her hands made tight fists in the sheets as I slid myself slowly inside of her.

My fingers went to her hips and then I slid the palm of my hand up along the knotted ridges of her spine. Steffie arched her back. I dug my clawed hands into the soft flesh of her shoulders.

I can still remember the way Steffie moaned for those first few seconds that I was slowly sliding the length of my cock deep inside her; the way her whole body tensed, the slow undulation of her back and her hips as though internally she was adjusting and accommodating me. Then, when I was deep inside her, our bodies joined, she hung her head so that her hair fell forward across her face like a veil and she swayed there, braced on her hands and knees with her breasts spilling from out of the cups of her corset. I didn't move for the longest time. I was savoring the sensations – the tight gripping feel of her pussy, the warmth and tautness of her. When I drew myself back and then thrust forward for the first time, we both groaned.

Suddenly the lines for me between sex and power blurred. Just moments before I was burning on pure lust and desire. Steffie was arched, spread, ready and very willing. But now, with myself deep inside her, I instinctively wanted more. *I wanted her to be a part of what happened next, not just a willing object for my own satisfaction.*

You get that right? As a woman there must have been plenty of times in your life when the sex became just about the man – you were there but were forgotten as he grunted single-mindedly towards his own release. It's a common complaint I hear a lot from women. So many other men just seem to rush towards their climax and disregard the lady…

Anyhow, in that moment with Steffie I suddenly realized. A door of understanding opened wide for me and I stepped through. Even in this most aggressive position, I didn't want the sex to be for my pleasure – *somehow I had to draw out Steffie's own orgasm.*

We began to move together, her body rocking and responding to each measured thrust of my hips. I was trying to read her movements, trying to understand what felt good for her. Each deep lunge was met by a throaty groan, but the short teasing thrusts of my cock seemed to spark new flares of energy from her. I began to tease her with shorter, faster strokes. My hands fisted into the tangles of her hair and I pulled so that her face was lifted and her head thrown back. I could see a part of our reflection in the mirror. Her mouth was wide open, and her eyes screwed tightly shut. I could see the tremble in her tensed arms and the more urgent sway of her breasts and they kept beat with the rhythm of my hips.

I told Steffie to imagine she was being watched by other men. I told her to visualize herself on her hands and knees in the middle of a spot-lit stage. Gathered around her in the smoke-filled shadows were strangers – other men – their eyes hungrily watching her, growling their appreciation for the beauty of her.

Steffie's breathing became sharper – more urgent, and she began to rock back on my cock, *using me for her pleasure.* Suddenly the whole dynamic had changed. I had found a secret key to her personality, and by turning that key I had hit upon the touchstone that elevated the sex we were sharing into something profoundly erotic.

Steffie wanted those men in her imagination to desire her. She wanted each of the strangers she was visualizing behind her closed eyes to be overcome with lust. She wanted them to see her cum.

Her movements became more frantic, more urgent and our bodies crashed together like we were racing towards the peak of a mountain top. Beads of sweat squeezed out across my brow and ran in rivulets down my chest. Steffie's body glistened with the satin sheen of her perspiration. Suddenly the breath was seizing in my throat and Steffie began to twist her hips. I let go of her hair and she tossed her head from side to side. We were rocking together like two people in a small boat on a raging sea. Steffie cried out and it was the sound of her release – a raw primeval sound without any coherent form; the sound of her plunging into the abyss.

I came an instant later, my own orgasm seemingly wrenched from me by the frantic convulsing grip of Steffie's pussy. I threw my head back, saw the ceiling sway and blur. Sweat stung my eyes and at last the breath I had been holding was torn from me in a sound like a growl…

That was the nature of our relationship in those early days Steffie and I shared together – more playfulness than serious BDSM lifestyle. In fact, it was as much about exploring each other's minds and desires than it was about dominance and submission. Those other aspects developed over time as Steffie's confidence and trust grew, and as her inhibitions were tenderly and thoughtfully explored and then peeled away.

I learned a lot from that relationship – and not all that I learned had anything to do with the art of being a Master. Much of it was about learning to be a man.

I learned about the importance of foreplay for a woman – the need to build a sense of desire through anticipation… and I learned about the value of exploring fantasy.

The key to releasing a woman's sexuality is to understand her secret fantasies.

I actually wrote that line down on a scrap of paper several years ago and put it in a desk drawer. I found the note today, the page a little dog-eared, the paper now faded. I read it again before I came to visit you tonight because I have been thinking about you.

A lot…

I can't say the relationship with Steffie ended too soon because it didn't, in hindsight. It ended at the exact right time. For me, I was soon to meet another young lady, someone thrilling and spectacular, and for Steffie… well I honestly don't know. I never saw her again but when we parted she said she was happy. I hope she is today…

But the memory of her still haunts me…

* * *

Look, I need to say something to you because I promised when I arrived that we would be honest with each other, right?

Well something's bothering me, and I feel you and I need to talk this through.

Here's my problem.

I still feel like you're looking at me like I'm Jason Luke the author.

I'm not. Not tonight. Not here with you.

Tonight I'm just a guy, and that's how I need you to think of me. Strip everything else away – the author profile and all the social media – and what remains is just a guy.

And you're a woman. We ought to be able to connect, and I want something deeper from this – and I want the same thing for you. We're both searching for something, right? I know I am. I still haven't found what I'm looking for, but I know what it is – I know what I want.

Refuge. Harmony.

Solace.

Respite – from the demons of my guilt; the flail of remorse that still stings when I recall the women I have hurt throughout the meandering course of my life because I was too young, too self-centered... too arrogant.

I'm not perfect and I'm not Jason Luke. Not twenty-four-seven.

Not tonight.

With you I just want to be me, and I want you to be the real you. Just give that much of yourself – even if it's for these few hours.

Okay?

Maybe you're searching for something too – some emotional or sensual fulfillment. Maybe that's why you invited me into your home. Perhaps it goes deeper than just the whim of erotic entertainment. Maybe we're searching for the same thing, coming at the issue from opposite directions; me as a writer and you as a reader. But we have common ground – we're people. Tomorrow we'll be alone again. You'll go your way and pick up another book. I'll begin writing again...

But tonight we can, between us, make a little magic; a firework of happiness in a dark, dark sky. That's got to be worth the effort, right?

Come on, there's other stories I want to share with you.

Are you ready for more?

I want to tell you about Emily.

* * *

Okay, I promised you another story about a woman named Emily, and I'll get to that in a moment. But first I want to ask you something.

What turns you on?

I've been watching you since I arrived, and the enigma of you enthralls me. I know women like to remain a little mysterious, but I simply cannot work you out.

I've come here to your secret place and all I have to seduce you with is my words. Somehow I think you're the kind of woman that needs more.

I don't imagine the fakery of flirtation would touch you. The whole superficial charade falls away too quickly to leave a profound effect.

No.

It would need something more.

How would Jason Luke seduce you?

We'd dance.

That's right. In your bedroom, or maybe in the living room; just you and I alone, with no one watching.

I'd find a radio station that plays old songs from the '80's and we'd slow dance together to old songs by the Rolling Stones so I could touch you, hold you and move against you. Then, when the music stopped, your face would be flushed, your heart tripping in your chest and your eyes glittering like gemstones.

I'd step close – slam shut the space between us and gaze into your eyes.

Can you imagine that? Can you picture the moment between us when we're standing, touching and our mouths are just inches apart?

It's all I can think about.

Everything would teeter for an instant. Would you draw away? Would your eyes become hectic?

Would you need me to take control?

I would. I couldn't help myself. My instinct would be to reach out confidently to cup your cheek in the palm of my hand. Suddenly time would stand still. I'd place my other hand over your heart to feel what you feel – and then I'd kiss you.

Properly.

Slowly. Very slowly.

For a very long time. *Until we both saw stars.*

* * *

Emily and I were friends and work colleagues before we became lovers. She was younger than me, and one of the most dazzling feminine contradictions I have ever encountered. In the work environment she was pleasant, professional and demure. But in private – Emily was a vivacious vixen: a bona fide nymphomaniac.

She was petite. Side by side she barely reached my shoulder. She had a slim waif-like figure that meant to most men she might have appeared quite unremarkable.

But to me, there was something wickedly arousing about her. It was the way she wore her jeans, the way she moved her hips when she walked and the bold, almost brazen way she made eye contact, like every time we spoke she was daring me to kiss her.

When we did eventually get together, it was at a work event – a presentation night hosted by one of the company's supplier clients. There were hundreds of people from competitor businesses across the city in attendance. Emily sat next to me and when the lights were dimmed in the auditorium and a video presentation began playing on the giant screen, I felt her body sway against mine, connecting us in the gloom from her hip all the way up to her shoulder. I sat quite still while my mind raced to consider the implications. Emily was incredibly sexy.

I wanted her.

Her hand slipped beneath the table, and then I felt her fingers drop into my lap. She was looking away, staring with rapt fascination at the big screen. Her touch crawled over my thigh and then came back higher until she was kneading my erection with her tiny hands through the tented denim of my jeans.

I leaned forward and propped my elbows on the table, resting my chin atop my clenched hands. There were a dozen other people around us, the table littered with empty plates. Waitresses were gliding around the room like ethereal ghosts, cleaning up after the dessert had been served. I stared at a middle-aged lady from a competitor store. She was sitting directly across from me. She must have sensed that I was watching her. She drew her attention away from the screen and flashed me a friendly smile. Then she saw Emily close against me and her intuition must have been aroused. Maybe there was some telltale sign in my face, or maybe she saw something in the way Emily's shoulder was moving. Her gaze turned into a glare – and then the lights came back on.

Emily removed her hand and sat up straight in her chair, casual and unhurried. The two women exchanged glances and something distinctly feminine and beyond my understanding passed between them. Emily's eyes flashed and then she turned to me and stared close into my face, her lips parted and glossy and her cheeks flushed.

"Let's go back to my place," she told me.

Emily rented an apartment just ten minutes from where we worked. The downstairs was a kitchen and living space. Upstairs were a couple of bedrooms and a compact bathroom.

We made it as far as the foyer.

She had been pensive and withdrawn in the drive back to her home. Now, suddenly, she was ravenous. She brushed against me like a sleek cat in the doorway and then pushed the door closed with her hip and threw herself into my arms. We kissed fiercely, breathless. My hands went to her ass as her arms locked around my neck.

We stumbled as far as the sofa and spent the rest of the evening on the carpeted floor, peeling away each other's clothes and making small murmured sounds of delight. Emily's kisses were like fire, the swirl of her tongue within my mouth wet and moist and alive.

I rolled her onto her back and unbuttoned her blouse. She lay with her legs apart unbuckling and unzipping her own jeans. I took one of her nipples into my mouth and she hissed through her teeth and then arched her back. I felt her hands entwine into the hair at the nape of my neck, clutching me to her while my free hand glided down across her belly and within the elastic of her lace panties.

Now that we were locked together, Emily seemed a willing passive partner. She groaned when the tips of my fingers brushed against the hard nub of her clit and then she groaned more deeply as my touch became more insistent, more demanding.

I let her nipple slip from my lips and lay on my side with my elbow propped beneath me. I studied Emily's face.

Her eyes were screwed tightly shut, her brow crinkled into a little furrow of concentration. There was heat and color rising on her cheeks and her mouth was open, her lipstick smudged by our kisses. My palm between her spread legs was pressing against her clit and I watched the changing play of her features and emotions as her arousal slowly grew, like rising music towards a crescendo. I felt the slick warm wetness of her in a rush and then two of my fingers slipped inside her pussy.

She was wearing red lace panties and my knuckles were tight bulges inside the sheer fabric, moving and manipulating as though I were fine tuning a beautiful instrument. For an instant Emily's eyes fluttered open. She gazed at me and her eyes were dreamy. Her mouth became a cunning, secret smile, and then changed again into a perfect 'O' as I filled her clenching pussy with another finger.

I kissed her again, this time more deliberately, in complete control. She was at my willing whim, and there was plenty I wanted from her.

The kiss lasted a long time and when we broke apart, both panting, I told Emily that for the night she was my submissive. I told her I expected her complete unquestioning obedience.

She nodded her head, suddenly solemn. I told her to get undressed.

I wanted her naked.

I led Emily into her kitchen. Nested around a wooden table were four chairs and a wall covered by vertical drapes. I asked Emily what was behind the drapes and she told me it was a set of sliding glass doors with a view through her neighbor's living room window.

I set a chair facing the drapes and ordered Emily to sit with her legs wide apart. I told her to pleasure herself. I wanted to watch her cum. Emily nodded and gnawed at her lip. Her right hand dipped spontaneously to the shaved mound of her pussy, and then she touched herself with several slow lingering caresses before pressing against her clit with her fingertips. I stood and watched her for several moments – and then drew the vertical blinds open.

For an instant Emily froze, like a shocked deer in the middle of a road, suddenly caught in the glare of headlights. There was a light on in a window of the facing house.

Emily made to flee from the chair but I snapped at her. I told her I wanted to watch her orgasm. The sooner she got herself off, the sooner the blinds would be closed.

She flashed me a venomous glare and then screwed her eyes tightly shut. Her face looked as though she were in some deep trance of concentration. Her nipples came taut and then her abdomen began to undulate as her tummy concaved with each deeply drawn breath.

Okay… I just need to stop here for a moment because I'm wondering if you notice a trend yet?

I'll come back to my story about Emily very soon, but this is important – important enough to share a secret with you.

I've always made it a rule in my **BDSM** experiences to insist my submissive pleasure herself before I ever attempt to bring her to orgasm.

Why?

Well how else will I know how to pleasure her – how best to touch her to bring her to release?

A woman's orgasm is hidden behind a million combination tumblers; what works for one woman *never, ever* works in exactly the same way for the next. Most guys might think they know how to pleasure a woman. And maybe they do.

A woman. *A single woman.*

But any guy who uses exactly the same techniques on every woman he ever tumbles into bed with is going to disappoint the majority of them.

I'm not smart. I'm just smart enough to know I need each lady's combination. It's the only way the sex can be mutually satisfying, after all.

Okay. Okay. I know – there's nothing worse than breaking off a good story just when it's about to get interesting. I'll come back to Emily and what happened during our first night together…

While Emily slowly rose towards the thrill of her release I studied her closely; the way she moved, and the little touches that seemed to turn her breath into soft gasps. She reached the brink at last and teetered there for over a minute. In that time she never breathed – the air became jammed in her throat so that when she went crashing through the thrash of her orgasm, she was panting and starved for air as if she had run to the end of a marathon finishing line.

She was like a limp rag doll in the chair, her arm dangling between her spread legs and one of her legs tapping a trembling beat against the floor. Her head lolled to the side, her eyes bleary as though she had just awaken. I drew the vertical drapes closed and took her languid hand.

Quietly, I led her up the stairs.

One bedroom was filled with cardboard boxes and in the other room was an unmade king-size bed. Emily moved like a sleepwalker. I positioned her at the foot of the bed and gently put pressure on her shoulders. She understood instinctively and sank to her knees before me.

I unzipped my jeans and stood perfectly still. Emily took me tentatively in her mouth and my hands went to the back of her head, guiding and instructing her with the pressure of my touch.

She was willing but lacked skill, and it took more patience than I had in order to finally control her throat gagging lunges into a more sedate, controlled rhythm. After a couple of minutes, I was still hard but no more aroused. I drew myself back from between her lips, wet and glistening and Emily sat back on her haunches, pouting her lips like a petulant child.

I ordered her to start again. Emily sulked for a moment longer and then she opened her mouth wide. Firmly, I cupped her face in my hands and then slowly pushed my hips forward until the hard swollen tip of my cock was resting on her tongue. Emily's eyes were enormous, fixed upon my face and her mouth filled with saliva. I held myself between her lips for a long moment and then inched myself deeper into her mouth.

Instinctively Emily's mouth clamped tight around the heat of my shaft. I gave her a sharp warning look, and her expression altered. She let out a long breath through her nose and the tension in her melted a little. I thrust slowly forward until I felt the tip of my cock brush against the back of her throat, and then withdrew myself quickly, before she gagged.

"Again." I said.

We repeated the process for several minutes until Emily understood that her mouth was being used for my pleasure. She became completely passive, and when her eyes at last closed and the final shreds of her resistance drained away, I began to rock my hips, at last able to enjoy the sensations as her tongue fluttered along my shaft and my cock became coated with the moist wetness of her desire to please.

In the back of her throat Emily was making little grunting noise of contentment – maybe satisfaction. Having surrendered entirely, she was suddenly perfectly pliant. I used her hungry mouth until I felt the first tingling thrill of my own desire begin to peak, and then drew back from her lips and stared, smiling, down into her eyes.

We drifted towards the bed and Emily stretched out on her back, looking to me for guidance and direction. I spread her legs with my hands and knelt before her. Her pussy was glistening with her own arousal, like dewdrops on a rose at dawn. I drew my tongue slowly along the soft smooth folds of her sex, and she went rigid in the grips of sudden sensitive desire.

I told Emily she could not come – and then I tortured her.

Her performance in front of the glass kitchen doors had taught me a great deal about how Emily brought herself to orgasm. With my tongue and the tips of my fingers I set about replicating her movements, alternating light and firm pressure, licking at the warm rush of her juices and drinking in the taste of her. She began to thrash upon the bed, starting with a gentle rock and rise of her pelvis as the need for her to come took hold. The rhythmic movements of her body became quickly more urgent. Quivering tension reached her legs and she became restless on the bed. Her head swished from side to side on the big pillows and then I felt her hands, hooked into claws, scratching at my shoulders. Her nails were like talons. They hooked into my flesh and then she threw back her head, her jaw locked tight and her eyes squeezed closed.

I stopped.

For an instant Emily laid frozen in that arched, strained pose – and then her eyes fluttered open and the breath she had been holding escaped in a long quivering gasp. She looked down between her open wide knees to where I was crouched, trembling, her expression bewildered and crestfallen.

I started again, drawing the button of her clit gently between my lips and at the same time slowly sliding one of my fingers inside her. Emily groaned. She was already close to the brink. Now she began to push her pussy against my mouth, slowly grinding and gyrating her hips to keep contact as my lips drew back, and I flickered my tongue gently across her. My touch was teasing, tantalizing – deliberately never applying enough pressure for long enough to trigger her orgasm. Emily started to sob with bitter frustration. It reached the point where I was literally forcing her to be aroused, despite her resistance. She was helpless… and I was merciless.

When I finally covered her with my body and the length of my cock slid deep between the aching wet folds of her pussy, Emily's body turned limp in my arms.

She asked me if she could come. I told her no.

"Not until I'm finished with you."

I took my time, savoring the feel of her firm resilient flesh beneath me, attuned to every single movement she made as I drove myself deep inside her. Her legs entwined around my ankles and one of her hands slipped down between our bodies, her fingers rubbing at her clit.

She lifted herself off the bed, driving upwards with her hips to meet each new thrust, encouraging me deeper. Her pussy clenched tight.

I buried my face in her neck and kissed her throat. Her hair was damp with her perspiration. I pressed my lips to her ear, so she could hear the rising tempo and urgency in my breathing. My senses became overwhelmed with the scent of her perfume and the aroma of sex that hung like a veil in the air. I immersed myself in it and then bit her shoulder, hard enough that she made a sound like a squeal that blended into a deep throaty moan.

I reached the verge of my own orgasm. My breath sounded hoarse in my own ears. My eyes were screwed shut. I hunted for Emily's mouth and when I felt the softness of her lips, I kissed her with a fierce blend of desire and passion.

When I came, Emily rode the waves with me, melting her body against mine, pressing forward where I pulled away and softening herself against the pressure of my chest so that we were completely connected, skin-on-skin from our feet to our lips.

It took a long time for me to return from the far distant place of release and profound emptiness. Emily was lying pliant and waiting beneath me. Her eyes were huge, her expression significant. I kissed her more tenderly and then lay beside her on the bed, still breathing hard. I gave her permission to come.

Emily's fingers flew gratefully between her spread legs. She was slick with the nectar of her own long-held arousal and the warm rush of my release. She closed her eyes. I propped myself up onto one elbow and casually drew one of her nipples into my mouth.

Emily touched herself tentatively for a few moments until her fingers were glistening with her moistness. She let out a long breath that became a gasp, and then her fingers turned into a blur – as though the moment could not be withheld for an instant longer.

Her orgasm left her broken – shattered into separate loose pieces.

It was a compelling, intimate moment to watch, as though I were stealing a look at a private piece of her very soul.

We spent the rest of the night together and in the morning I followed her into work. The day was fraught with significant looks, secret touches and hushed, flirting conversation. I trailed her back to her apartment that evening, and we went driving up into the mountains in my car.

The night was warm and filled with stars. We parked in a clearing just off the road that had a view down across the lights of the city. The only sound was the buzzing of insects. I ordered Emily to get undressed and then she perched herself precariously sideways in her seat and leaned across the center console of the car to take my cock in her mouth.

After the night before, she was timid, and I put the palm of my hand between her shoulder blades to encourage her to take me deep down her throat.

I sat back in the bucket seat, staring at the cabin light. Emily was making pleasant sucking sounds, and I could feel myself become fully hard. I reached around behind Emily and slid my hand between her thighs. Her pussy was already wet – the teasing play throughout the day had lingering side-effects. When the tip of my finger slipped between the folds of her sex, she stopped sucking my cock and laid her cheek on my lap, looking at me.

I began to slowly fuck her with my finger, encouraged by her moans and little gasps of delicious arousal. She began to rock back and forth slowly, her back arched, the long tendrils of her dark hair teasing across my cock like the brush of feathers.

After several minutes the air was rich with the musky scent of her aroma. She wrapped her hand around the base of my cock and began to stroke me slowly. I used the wetness of her pussy to glide my fingers in tight circles over her clit, and she shuffled her thighs as wide apart as she could in the confined space.

"I want to fuck you – over the hood of the car."

Emily did not flinch. In fact, she nodded her head in willing agreement. We stepped out of the car and the warm air wrapped itself around us like a blanket. Emily's body was pale in the moonlight, ethereal and slim as a wisp. I bent her over the hood of the car and spread her legs wide. Emily splayed her fingers wide on the paintwork as though to hold herself steady. My cock swiped slowly along the pouting lips of her pussy and then I slid inside her, coming up onto the balls of my feet for balance and leverage.

The grip of her pussy was like sliding inside a silken glove. The tightness of her was accentuated by her wetness. I held myself still, deep within her and Emily gave a little contented gasp of encouragement.

I gave Emily a playful slap on the bottom as I was driving my hips into her. She turned her head and glanced at me over her shoulder. Her mouth was open, her eyes slanted with a look of sloe-eyed sexuality.

It occurred to me then that we were physically perfect for each other. The length of Emily's legs, the petite shape of her figure was a perfect match – all the parts that mattered fitted together perfectly so that the sex we shared seemed entirely natural and unforced.

A car drove past, the headlights playing through the veil of low shrubs and dappling us with light for a sweeping moment. The car drove on without slowing, the engine changing down through the gears as the vehicle tackled the peak of the mountains. The sound finally faded into the night just as Emily began to moan, telling me she was on the verge of coming. One of her hands snaked down between her spread legs and found the sensitive tip of her clit. I could feel the brush of her other fingers against the end of my shaft. In the wetness of her arousal, our bodies made soft slapping sounds.

I told Emily not to come, and increased the tempo of my thrusts. I could feel the forced restraint of her now, like she was clenching her body, holding herself in check with a desperate will. I dug my hands into her hips and pulled her hard onto my cock so that I was completely inside her. She threw back her head and I snatched at her shoulder then slid my hand around until it was wrapped around her throat. I was grunting, growling – racing quickly to the point of orgasm. Having Emily held, pinned and helpless in my grip was a turn on. She was allowing me to use her – welcoming and encouraging me.

At the moment before I began to thrill, I gave Emily permission to enjoy her own orgasm, and our rhythm broke down as we both went in search of release. Emily began to push back against me, and the thrust of my hips became savage. Each crashing together of our bodies filled the air with grunts and passion-fuelled groans. Emily arrived at the abyss before me; her body wrenched and then went stiff. I kept driving myself deep inside her. She hunched her shoulders, and then gasped – did the same thing two more times – and then went very still. She was panting, tumbling down from her high and struggling to catch her breath.

I sensed the instant when I had reached the trigger of my own orgasm – that split-second of no return. Emily sensed it too. She came off the hood of the car, turned and dropped to her knees in the same movement with her mouth wide open. I threw back my head, literally saw stars – and then came hard across her tongue.

During the drive back to her apartment we talked quietly about the evening, and Emily revealed that the fantasy of a car full of men stopping and wanting to fuck her had tipped her over the edge, down into the spiral of a powerful orgasm. But she was like that as a person and as a sex partner.

Emily was a free spirit. She taught me spontaneity and in return I taught her some aspects of the BDSM lifestyle. In truth, BDSM was never for Emily. She was as keen to try breast-play as she was bondage – as enthusiastic to try a threesome as she was orgasm denial. She was a sexual thrill-seeker. The relationship was like a shooting star; a blinding flash of light followed by a slow dimming decline.

Into nothingness.

We didn't break up, we just drifted apart. I was offered a new job with a rival business and took it, always drawn to meeting new people by the lure of the BDSM lifestyle and the search for a compatible partner. Emily went seeking her own new sexual delights. I don't know that she ever found the utopia she was looking for. Last time I heard from her she was miserable in a marriage with children. It seemed a sad way for such a sensual woman to settle – like a sleek and beautiful wild animal trapped behind the bars of a cage.

* * *

Alright. I've done a lot of talking, but I have just as many questions I want to ask you as I have erotic stories to share. You see I *really* need to understand what things you find sexy. But there is one question that simply cannot wait any longer – something special I have wanted to ask you ever since we got here.

It's important to me so I'd like you to think about your answer.

What *is* erotica to you? Have you ever asked yourself that question? Have you ever sat down and considered which single act defines erotica in your own mind?

Not sex. Erotica.

It's something I think about a lot. Maybe it's because of the writing I do, but I've thought long and hard about this question and do you know what I've decided?

Shuffle closer, I'm going to whisper this because, for a man, what I am about to share will probably surprise you.

Are you listening?

Okay – to me, the act of kissing a woman's throat is the absolute definition of erotica. That single action encapsulates the essence of the concept in my mind because it contains so much – promise, anticipation, intimacy...

Have you ever had a man kiss your neck – trail his lips down along the soft tender flesh of your throat?

Of course you have, right?

But have you ever thought about it – thought in depth about how much is happening in that fleeting instant of contact?

He is close, either standing behind or in front of you, and his hands are touching your body. You're so close that you can feel the heat of each other. Your head is thrown back, or inclined to the side, and your eyes are closed. Your mouth is open, your skin alive and tingling with a sizzle of so many sensations; the feel of his stubbled jaw, the musky man-smell of him, the soft growling sound he makes in the back of his throat...

It's the moment where intimacy and erotica blend, and where a defining moment can lead in so many directions.

It's the sensual time before sex, and yet the tantalizing time after the spark of desire has first been ignited. It's seductive without being graphic. It's all about touch, taste, smell and sound – the erotic cocktail of senses needed to seduce a woman.

Try it for me.

Touch your neck lightly – as lightly as you can with the bare tips of your fingers... trail them down across your neck and throat. Imagine it's me standing behind you, right now, holding you close. Think about the touch of your fingers being like the fire of my sensual kisses.

Can you feel it? Can you feel your skin come tingling alive?

Did your mouth open just a little?

Now slide your hand down to your breast. Imagine my fingers, gentle and exploring – touching you *the way you want to be touched*. The way you wish a man would know to touch you.

Breathe deeply.

Intimate. Erotic.

You're such a good girl for me.

* * *

Now that we've met; now we've becoming comfortable with each other and I'm here alone with you... *are you disappointed?*

Does the image of Jason Luke measure to this reality we're sharing?

You see I'm talking to you right now in the same way I would talk in everyday life, when I'm with any other woman. There's no passages of eloquent flowing prose, no lyrical metaphors... not even a contrived plotline or a story arc. It's just us, and I figure that might be a let down for you.

Some people read my books because of the language – the way I describe scenes – and I realize this must be a very different reality you're experiencing. It's just me, uncensored and unfiltered. I actually feel unarmed – unable to hide behind character conversation and all those neat things that writers use to create a sense of atmosphere.

Instead you've got me, alone with you in your private place, and I figure an exotic location with a compelling hero right now might just be a lot more appealing than listening to the real me.

I hope you don't really feel that way. I hope so far I've been all you expected: entertaining at least. I am enjoying our time together, *but I can't seem to shake the vision of watching you pleasure yourself.*

I said earlier that every woman has a fantasy.

Well men do too…

Touch yourself.

Do it – not because I'm commanding you, but because I'm *releasing* you – giving you permission to free yourself from inhibitions… allowing you to be yourself with me watching you.

Touch yourself because you want to, and because I want to watch you.

We've reached that stage now, haven't we? I feel like I can share almost anything with you – and I want you to feel the same way. I don't want barriers of self-consciousness to inhibit you for a moment more.

So touch yourself. Right now.

Slide your fingers down between your spread legs and let yourself relax. Draw your fingertips across the smooth skin of your inner thigh and then let them meander slowly higher. Take your time. Tease yourself. Draw out the moment for as long as you want – there's no hurry. We've got plenty of time. I want you to enjoy the delicious pleasure of feeling aroused and reacting to that urge in complete privacy – in complete safety.

Because it's just you and me alone here, and I'm watching you from the shadows. No one else will know. You have some of my secrets, and now I want to share this intimate pleasure with you. It will be something to take with me when I leave tonight. Something I can always savor and remember.

Say, 'yes Sir.' Whisper it as your fingers glide across the sensitive flesh of your pussy. Say 'yes, Jason.'

If I could touch you right now, I'd start with your shoulders, standing very close behind you so that our bodies were brushing against each other – so that I could feel the heat of you against me.

Could you imagine that?

Could you imagine standing in a shadow struck room, maybe with just a little pale light filtering in through the windows? The house would be quiet and we would be alone. I'd appear from out of the gloom. You'd smell my aftershave first, then sense that I was nearby.

I'd reach for you, pull you back against me and then begin to caress your shoulders.

Not massage. Caress. This would be sensual, provocative… the touch of my fingers suggesting that I wanted more from you.

How would you respond?

Would you close your eyes, throw your head back and gift me the long soft tender flesh of your throat? Would your breathing hitch? And if one of my arms wrapped around your waist and drew you close to me, would that be all right?

I can hear your breathing turn husky in the back of your throat and feel little pieces of you melting.

Shhhh.

It's okay. I want you to relax. I want you to slip into fantasy. We're sharing this together, you and I. It's intimacy made sensual. Go with it.

Imagine me gliding my hand slowly – very slowly – up over your body until I have one of your breasts cupped possessively.

Would you like that?

Lean against me. Sway back. It's perfectly okay. I want to feel you closer to me, and I want to be able to draw my lips down along your throat and smell the lingering scent of your perfume, and that first musky hint of deeper feminine desire.

Our bodies would sway slowly, pressed hard against each other, moving as one. You'd sense my need and, like dancers, I'd guide you with careful touches, encouraging you towards slow simmering arousal – sensing those parts of your body that begin to catch fire and salving them with cool fingers until my hands and our bodies were moving with a will of their own.

What would make your knees go weak? That's what I want to know.

Would it be the first passionate kiss that melts on your lips and somehow touches your soul… or would it be the hungry look in my eyes; that look that says I want to devour you?

Let yourself go.

I've got you…

* * *

I've always favored orgasm control as a way to discipline and punish submissives. I've never leaned towards the more corporal aspects of the lifestyle's punishment regimes. In fact, if *you* came to me for personal training, I'd control your orgasms as a way of instilling obedience in you to follow my every command.

How would you handle that, do you think?

Does the thought of submitting yourself for training by a Master arouse you?

Could you imagine what it might be like?

Whilst I don't live the lifestyle anymore, *and I haven't for quite some time,* I admit there are still moments in my life when I miss the interplay and dynamic that stems from a BDSM relationship.

Let's explore this, you and I. Let's have a quiet little discussion about why so many women find the idea of submitting sexually to a man appealing. I'd like to know your thoughts. I'd like to get a better understanding of what makes a woman want to submit and surrender her body willingly to a man.

What do you think? Is the fascination born from boredom with a man who is an inept lover… or is it some deeper sensory instinct − an urge to simply feel more feminine, more desired in the bedroom?

Is submission something you have ever actively considered… *has the idea ever crept into your sexual fantasies?*

Have you ever wondered what it would be like to surrender your mind, body and soul to a man?

You would look so very pretty wearing a collar.

Do you know that? Well you would.

Not anything bulky; nothing brash or overstated, that just wouldn't suit you, and I doubt it's your style any more than it is mine. No, for you the collar I'd select would be something very elegant − a piece that stated simply that you were owned… something you could wear every day and night as a secret reminder.

I do apologize if I am being too confronting. I have a habit of doing that, you know, so please forgive me. I tend to ask very direct and sometimes personal questions. I don't mean to – I simply have a genuine curiosity about other people and I rarely have the time for idle chatter, so my questions tend to be pointed – probing.

You don't have to say anything. I don't want you to feel uncomfortable, not when we have spent such a lovely time in each other's company. I don't want to ruin this time by making you feel awkward.

Well... okay, maybe I want you to feel a *little* awkward. I mean that's a good thing right? You know you are alive when you're taken just a little ways outside of your comfort zone.

It *is* a good thing.

So go with it...

* * *

Not all of my stories I want to share with you are about women I had sex with... although they are all about women... and sex...

You see there was this one woman I met named Karen. I never had sex with her, but we did have a frank and animated conversation – the kind of chat that anyone overhearing would have felt uncomfortable listening to.

We met at a local café and at the time Karen was probably thirty-five? Maybe thirty-seven...

Anyhow, we had been introduced through a mutual friend. I was still on my search for a compatible submissive woman with whom I could form a long-term relationship, and Karen was an experienced submissive who had just come *out* of a long-term relationship.

She was a slim-built woman with auburn hair.

Auburn... do people still say that – or do they say reddish-brown? I'm not sure, but you get the picture.

She had a tattoo of handcuffs on the inside of her right wrist and a thin strip of leather, knotted tight around her throat. She was wearing a long flowing loose-fitting dress and walking funny.

Yeah, really. It wasn't quite a limp. It was more of a pained, uncomfortable gait. I shook her hand when she came through the front door of the café, and we sat together in a corner booth. Once the waitress had gone, we started chatting about all those forgettable things that are small-talk until I asked her about her experiences in the lifestyle as a submissive woman.

Karen had seen every aspect of a submissive's life – the highlights and the lowlights. Her most recent Master had put her in a car with several men and given them all permission to fuck her during a long drive home. Apparently, half-way to their destination she fled from the car, humiliated and furious at the way her man had treated her… and that was the end of their relationship.

Other Masters she had served had been more considerate – too considerate apparently. The fine line between contentment and frustration was very fine indeed. I got the impression that Karen was looking for someone who would be firm, but without using pain as punishment.

And then a bizarre thing happened.

We started negotiating her submission to me.

I say bizarre because at the time it was. Now, with hindsight and more experience, I realize that Karen was a thoughtful, experienced submissive who knew what she wanted from a relationship. She wasn't going to go willingly to just any man who showed an interest; this was her submission she was offering and she wanted to be sure the man she surrendered to was worthy.

Smart lady.

But at the time it was like we were negotiating the sale of a house. The entire conversation was about likes, dislikes, and what we could accept. We tried to find middle ground. We chatted in an amiable way but Karen had a list – yes an actual handwritten list – of all the things she wanted to know from her potential Masters… how punishments would be handed out, what she would be expected to wear, how she would be required to behave in certain situations, as well as some specific hard limits.

I, on the other hand, was a little more instinctive. I didn't see the point in contracts or agreements because the relationship – like every other relationship – would always hinge on a majority vote of one. If either person was unhappy or unsatisfied, the relationship just didn't work, and that seemed particularly true in the BDSM lifestyle.

Anyhow, the waitress started hanging around a little more often and a little longer than was necessary. I'm sure she had overheard some aspects of our conversation and had become intrigued.

Karen sensed it too. She flashed the young woman a venomous glare and declared to me in a voice that was louder than necessary:

"I'm sorry. You probably noticed I was limping when I arrived, and since then I've had a hard time sitting still. It's because I had my clitoris pierced a couple of days ago and it's still tender."

I shit you not! That's what she said in the middle of the café on a busy Saturday morning.

The waitress disappeared and we did not see her again.

Karen wore the leather strap around her neck for a specific reason. She said it was a subtle message to others in the lifestyle that she was submissive but without a Master. It *was* a subtle message. If she hadn't told me, I, for one, would never have made the connection.

When it came down to it, Karen knew a lot more about BDSM than I probably ever will.

I have never been an expert on the lifestyle.

Never.

Karen knew the 'craft' of the lifestyle, and regularly attended social gatherings with likeminded people. I, on the other hand, had never mixed with others who enjoyed BDSM. I'd always done my own thing, made my own rules and I was perfectly happy that way. I didn't feel I needed to mix with others on a social level. What I was doing worked for me and the ladies I trained, and I needed nothing more. I never have.

There's no right or wrong way to engage in BDSM play. As long as it's safe, sane, and consensual... well you've probably heard the expression before...

Anyhow, I'm getting distracted. Sorry, my mind does that sometimes. My thoughts go off in a direction and my mouth follows. The point of telling you about Karen is this: she was a confident in-control woman who enjoyed the submissive lifestyle, without compromising her wants and needs. I respected her for that. To some men I am sure her confidence and knowledge would have been intimidating.

At last! Now I'm finally coming to my point...

Think about your own life. Maybe you're in a relationship with a man and you would love to explore the BDSM lifestyle with him – but you can't understand why he is so reluctant.

Sound familiar...?

Believe me when I tell you that a guy's sexual confidence hangs by a thin thread. You've been reading about the BDSM lifestyle. You know the language and maybe some of the sexual positions and aspects of submission too.

Compared to your man, you're well-researched.

Your guy, on the other hand, most likely knows little or nothing at all about BDSM.

That's damned intimidating for a guy. What if he makes a fool of himself in front of you?

What if he doesn't measure up in your eyes to the epic performances of all those erotic romance heroes you read about?

A lot of women assume a dominant, confident attitude to sex is something every man automatically inherits. They don't.

Just because a man can hammer in a nail, does not mean he's qualified as a carpenter.

* * *

I know what you're doing.

You're sitting, listening to me, but in the background, beneath the sound of my voice, your mind is playing back over our conversation and you're wondering if anything I have said contained some deeper, more significant meaning, right?

Right.

Well it didn't... but somehow I don't think that's going to stop you from analyzing everything word-for-word. I feel like you do that a lot, actually.

I get the impression that you'll often find yourself playing back over conversations wondering to yourself, 'What did that person *really* mean?'

Do you know what I'm talking about? I can't see whether you're nodding to yourself from over here.

Do you think that might also be why you tend to keep people at bay when you first meet them: why you're reserved and unwilling to give away too much of yourself until that person proves themselves genuine?

Are you nodding again?

I'm asking the question of you because I'm curious, but also because I feel that you and I, over the course of just a short time, have got something going here – some kind of a growing bond of understanding, and maybe even trust. It feels like I've known you all my life, and that's a little bit exciting because I know how naturally wary and reserved you are about people until you really get to know them.

How did it happen? How did we get to this place where I would call you a friend, in just a short time talking to each other?

Maybe it's because you're such a good listener. Or maybe it's because this intimate conversation we're having right now is good for both of us in its own way…?

Crazy… but a good kind of crazy, don't you think?

* * *

Look, there's another woman I really want to tell you about.

Her name was Christine and I met her at a time in my life after I had enjoyed some good long-term experiences with submissive women, but I was, at that moment, between relationships.

Christine came into my life at just the right time – never as a potential long-term partner, but as one of those people you encounter briefly whom you connect with on a singular level.

For Christine and me it was sex. Just sex. Outside of the bedroom we didn't have a lot in common and nor did either of us try to bridge the gap. We were happy with the simplicity of the arrangement. It was an *'ask no questions'* understanding. For all I knew when she left my apartment, Christine went home to a husband and three kids. I never asked, and she never offered to tell me.

Oh. Do you mind if I pace? I do that a lot while I'm thinking. Somehow it makes it easier to talk, to gather my thoughts into some kind of coherent order. I really want to tell this story properly because in a way, my encounter with Christine is one of the reasons you and I are having this private conversation right now. Inadvertently, Christine was responsible for me writing erotica.

So… um, the pacing thing…? You don't mind do you?

I met Christine through my work at the time. I went to her home after hours to interview her for a kind of client satisfaction survey. It was a questionnaire that took about forty-five minutes to complete.

When I rang her front doorbell, there was no answer. I waited for a few minutes on her front porch and then went around to the side of the home. There was a shoulder-high steel gate. I pulled it open and walked into the backyard of the house.

Christine was in her swimming pool, just wading across to the steps. She saw me, and her face lit up into a particularly friendly smile. She waved and called out a greeting. I watched her climb out of the pool. She was wearing a lemon yellow bikini that looked good against the color of her tan. She padded across the tiled surround and shook my hand. Droplets of water clung to her lashes like sparkling jewels.

"I wasn't expecting you," she said. *"I thought it would be someone else."*

Hmmm...

Now I'm not the smartest guy in the world, but I do know when a woman is lying, when she makes a mistake, and when she deliberately tells a blatant lie because she wants you to know she is lying but finds it easier to tell than a brazen truth. This was one of those.

Christine knew it would be me visiting – my secretary had called and confirmed the appointment at lunchtime.

I kept my expression neutral while Christine toweled her hair dry. Her eyes were slanted with sexuality, her lips pressed into a pout like she was anticipating a kiss. She excused herself for a minute and went back to the edge of the pool for her sunglasses, then stood, with the late afternoon sun directly behind her, and ran the towel slowly over her legs and across her breasts. Her nipples were hard, poking through the damp fabric of her tiny top and the bottoms of the bathers were so transparent I could clearly see the cleft of her sex through the material.

Christine was a shaver... or maybe a waxer...

She asked me if there was anything I would like, delivering the question from under hooded eyes, her words loaded with innuendo.

I said nothing.

We had met a week before at my office where I had spent a couple of hours talking to her about our product range. She was polite and curious – maybe just a little flirty – but she certainly was not provocative. She was attractive, educated, and well spoken.

Suddenly now she was something else entirely.

She rested her hand on my forearm and drew me through a set of glass doors, out of the sunlight and into the shade and gloom of a spacious kitchen. She smelled of chlorine and suntan lotion.

She went to the refrigerator and bent from the waist to search the lower shelves. The material of her swimmers rucked tightly up around the cheeks of her bottom.

Okay... so you get it, right? Christine, because of some unknown attraction, or maybe some unknown desperation, was coming onto me. I'll skip the rest of the prequel and move the story along, okay?

We tumbled into her big bed and Christine lay on her back. She was thirty-four when we met, with surgically enlarged breasts that pointed at the ceiling and natural blonde hair...

I peeled the damp bottoms of her bikini off and asked her what aroused her.

It turned out that Christine had two fantasies. In the first, she was a naughty teenage girl away at some kind of summer camp. She imagined her instructor catching her masturbating and then the man in her fantasies proceeded to punish her by bending her over the bed and fucking her roughly from behind.

Okey-dokey. No problems, I decided. In fact it fitted with my own fascination for domination and submission

But there was a problem with the second fantasy. I pride myself on being able to please a woman, but with Christine I met my Waterloo. Her second fantasy was to be lost in a forest. Suddenly the vines of a tree wrapped themselves around her wrists and her ankles, restraining her so she could not move. Then... and I am not making this up... another vine appeared from out of the tree and impregnated her with 'tree semen'.

What the fuck...?

I stared into her eyes and looked for signs of madness then said in a firm voice, *"Welcome to Camp Jason, you naughty girl!"*

* * *

I asked Christine to show me how she pleasured herself. She peeled away her bikini top and ran her hands over the magnificent mounds of her breasts and then glided her fingers down between her parted thighs. I watched with avid attention.

Christine told me she needed *a lot* of pressure on her clit in order to orgasm, and then she began to touch herself. One of her fingers dipped between the lips of her pussy and reappeared slick and glistening with her juices. Christine began to rub her clit and slowly – very slowly – her breathing became deep and sonorous and her eyes closed. Her lips parted and she licked them with the tip of her tongue.

"Help me," she said softly.

I took over massaging her pussy, applying firm pressure with the tips of my fingers across her clit. Christine cooed but begged for more. I pressed more firmly. Christine's lips curled into a languid seductive smile, but still she needed more pressure. By this point I was pressing down on her clit so firmly I thought I might break her, but for Christine it still was not enough and I realized I had to find another way to arouse her. If I didn't, I was going to end up with the muscled forearms of a pro tennis player.

"Show me again," I insisted. Christine nodded bravely and her head kind of drooped to the side. She took a deep breath and began to push down with her palm and at the same time thrust upwards with her hips so that the sound was a slapping collision of her sensitive bud against her hand. It went on for a long time until Christine was panting and gasping for air. I watched with a mixture of fascination and mortification until at last she began to squeal.

I edged away on the mattress and gave her space. Her body began to undulate and writhe and then the sound of her coming rose higher and higher in pitch. She was arched off the bed, frozen with her shoulders and heels digging into the mattress, but the rest of her body elevated off the sheets. The squeal reached a crescendo and then suddenly she collapsed panting and gulping fresh air into her lungs.

Either Christine had just orgasmed, or she had pressed down so hard on her clit that she had fractured her own wrist.

* * *

After that first afternoon together in her bedroom, Christine and I never met again at her home; she always came to my apartment, and always of an evening.

Normally when she would arrive, we would engage in a few minutes of small-talk and then, as if by some telepathic understanding, we would drift into the bedroom.

Sometimes she would arrive angry and flustered with a sense of agitated restlessness about her. On those occasions she was especially passionate. Christine gave great angry sex. But normally our time in the bedroom followed fairly simplistic dominant - submissive principals; she was willing and obedient, but never *enthralled*.

Do you know what I mean by that?

Maybe it's not the right word, but it's the best one I can come up with sitting here chatting to you. I just mean that whilst Christine was very good at playing the role of the obedient submissive, it was never something that came from her soul. There was never a moment where she spoke during sex that was pure passion. Everything she whispered or begged or sobbed was delivered with the skill of an accomplished actress playing a part, rather than from her heart.

For me it took the edge off our encounters... but from a physical point of view they remained spectacular. Unfortunately I was looking for a deeper connection. It's one of the reasons the relationship was so one-dimensional. I just wanted more... and Christine, I suppose, wanted something else entirely.

The last time we had sex was a Monday evening. Christine arrived just minutes after I had come home from work. She came up the stairs to the front door of my apartment while I was sitting outside, waiting for her. It was hot and there was a small breeze. I heard her before I saw her and recognized the clap-clap of her high-heels on the staircase beneath me.

When she stepped up onto my level, she was in a smoldering rage, her eyes flashing and her cheeks flushed. She brushed straight past me and stood, shaking with fury, in my kitchen. I followed her inside.

She told me she only had an hour. I told her that would be more than enough time. She undressed right there in the kitchen. She was wearing a long dress that clung tightly to the curves of her figure. She peeled it off like it was a second skin and stood in white lace lingerie, her irritated breathing making her breasts bulge and swell from the cups of her bra.

"Do you want my pussy?"

That's exactly what she asked me, and made a gesture with her hand like she was waving a wand. Her panties disappeared like magic.

We didn't make it to the bedroom. I bent Christine over the kitchen counter and she stood spread legged and folded forward at the waist. She pressed her cheek against the countertop and I moved behind her. Her pussy was already wet, and when she heard me unzip my jeans her hands bunched into tight fists.

We both groaned that first moment I entered her. The breath escaped through Christine's clenched teeth like a hiss of steam and her pussy went into immediate contractions, gripping with the rhythm of her racing pulse. I held myself still inside her and put one hand in the broad of her back to hold her still.

For the first few moments of long patient strokes, neither of us made another sound. It was as if we were both holding our breath, or maybe we were both waiting for an instant of inspiration. I slid my hands down until I had hold of Christine's hips and she began to slowly rock back with her body to meet each new lunge.

Suddenly, and without provocation, I slapped her ass – hard. The sound was a crack like a gunshot and the cheek of Christine's bottom turned bright red. She flinched and then cried out, more, I think, in shock than in pain.

I slapped her other cheek with the same force and then took a fierce fistful of her hair, pulling so that her face was lifted up off the countertop and she had to brace herself with her arms.

I told her she was a naughty girl and that I was displeased with her. I told her that she had to be punished, and then I slapped her bottom again, holding her hair like reins in my free hand.

Christine bucked and twisted against the pinning force of my cock inside her. She let out a hoarse growl of giddy arousal and clenched her jaw, begging me to teach her a naughty girl lesson she would never forget.

I froze for a moment and then pulled my cock from within her pussy. Christine deflated and groaned.

I ordered her onto her knees and barked at her to put her hands behind her back. When she had complied, I circled around, critically inspecting her submissive positioning and posture like a parade-ground drill sergeant.

We'd never really gone much for the discipline aspects of BDSM in the past – we were both pretty much satisfied with the spontaneous combustion of our physical attraction. That alone had sustained us. Now I decided it was time to introduce a new aspect to our encounters.

I cupped my hand under Christine's chin, lifting her eyes to mine and told her that submission was about willing surrender. I told her that she should leave her personal problems with her clothes at the front door. I told her that our time together was not for anything other than my pleasure and that *her* pleasure should be derived from satisfying me. Then I told her that good girls were rewarded with orgasms and bad girls went home with an empty feeling of frustration.

She told me she wanted to be a good girl in the baddest possible way. I didn't understand that to be truthful but it sounded kinda cool. It also sounded – for the very first time – like something that seemed *real*. Passionate. There was no acting. Her words were genuine. In that instant I realized that the role-play, which had characterized Christine's submissive poses, suddenly burned away like a morning mist and she *became* submissive. The look in her eyes changed. The vacant distance of her gaze blossomed into something soulful.

I took Christine again on the kitchen floor on her hands and knees with her perfect ass high in the air. She looked at me from over her shoulder. Her breasts had spilled free from the cups of her bra. Her nipples were hard and pointed. She balanced on one arm and reached behind herself to stroke her hand along the moistening slit of her pussy as if in invitation. For a moment I watched her touch her fingers to her clit, then provocatively open herself up to my gaze, wide and wet. Her hair hung in a long blonde cascade over her shoulder, almost brushing the floor tiles, and the look in her eyes became smoldering.

She touched at her lips with the tip of her tongue and then her hand on her pussy caressed the cheek of her ass. She shifted her weight a little, changed the tilt of her hip, and her hand reached down again to her pussy, rubbing herself in long slow strokes.

I stayed on my feet with my legs spaced wide apart behind her. Christine planted the palms of her hands on the floor and raised her hips up to meet me. I slid deep inside her and the air came from her lungs in a deep sigh that was significant. Her head turned to the side, and we made eye contact. She began to gasp softly as I started thrusting inside her with long, slow, measured strokes. I was rocking my whole body, swinging forward and bending at the knees, with one hand clutching at the kitchen counter to maintain my balance and to add weight to each thrust. I filled her completely and Christine melted into a long throaty groan that was raw with desire.

After several minutes I could feel the first far away tingles of my orgasm. I dropped down onto my knees and Christine lowered her body so that her elbows were on the ground, her fingers splayed wide on the tiles as if to give her purchase. The tendrils of her hair swept the ground with every rock of her body and her firm milky-white breasts swayed. I had one hand in the small of her arched back and she began to meet the beat of my thrusts – but in a way that was quite different to our previous sexual encounters. Now she was matching my rhythm as if to maximize the pleasurable sensations from her pussy rather than meeting each thrust to speed herself to orgasm. Something had changed, ignited by the tone of my voice and my attitude. Christine was giving herself wholly to me.

Her rocking became more determined. She took one of her fingers and sucked the tip into her mouth. My hands slid up around her waist and clamped around her body. Her skin felt warm and tingling.

Her enthusiasm drove me quickly to the edge of orgasm. Christine seemed to sense my rising urgency. She reached back to strum her fingers across her clit. The air was filled with the sounds and scents of sex.

On the very brink of exploding I withdrew myself from her pussy and rocked back on my heels, my cock achingly hard, the lips of Christine's pussy flared wide and swollen. Her fingertips across her clit were a blur. I watched her for a long moment, my cock twitching with my own insatiable need.

I drew Christine to her feet and bent her body forward. She folded herself almost in half, balanced on her heels, her long slender legs perfectly straight and parted slightly. Her head was down around near her knees. She reached back and dug her hands into the cheeks of her ass for a moment until I was buried, once again, deep within her pussy.

I was gentle for a few seconds, my fingers gripping the tops of her thighs. Christine reached down with one hand and made a tee-pee with her fingertips on the floor to balance herself, and with her other hand she gripped her ankle. I imagined her eyes tightly closed and her mouth wide open in a gasp of pleasure. She began to sway gently on my cock and each sound from her throat was a blend of cried delight and the strain of her physical position.

It sounded like I was touching a secret part of her soul.

Christine's wicked gasps were incredibly arousing. Every whisper, every growling husk in the back of her throat spoke of pure sensual pleasure that went beyond the physical and seemed to elevate the eroticism of the moment.

Her hand around her ankle ran up along the taut length of her thigh and then disappeared for a moment. I heard the sound of her sucking her fingers and then felt her touch between her legs. She was pleasuring herself, bending her knees just a little to reach her clit. I wished that I could have seen her face – more than anything else I wanted that. I wanted to see the dreamy pleasure in her eyes mirroring the sounds in her throat.

I took my hands from her thighs, thrust just a few more times and then withdrew myself from her pussy.

Christine looked back over her shoulder. She saw my glistening cock and her smile became deliciously debauched. She reached out for me, took my length in her hand, sinking down onto her knees at the same time and opening her mouth wide.

I was beginning to sway. The edges of my vision burst into swirling light.

I stared down and watched Christine's mouth engulf me, her lips and her hand working in practiced unison along my shaft until the flesh there seemed to burn and prickle with unrestrained urge. Christine hooded her eyes, alternating her gaze between the sight of my cock disappearing between her pouting lips, and the rapt expression on my face. I felt my eyes sear her with burning desire as her mouth made exquisite love to my cock until at last I could hold back not a moment longer.

I erupted deep in her mouth and she gulped and slurped hungrily until I had nothing more – nothing at all left to give.

Christine had been a *very* good girl for me and my good girls always got rewarded. I perched her on the edge of the kitchen countertop and she parted her legs wide, then leaned back with her head resting against the wall.

I went down on one knee and kissed her swollen clit. I heard Christine sigh. The lips of her pussy were flared and swollen with her arousal, the flesh of her shaved sex reddened. My lips slid down to the wetness welling within her and I lapped at her juices hungrily. Christine wrapped one hand into the hair at the back of my head and braced her balance with the other. I reached up with one hand and teased her nipple while the other hand held her knees wide apart. Christine threw back her head and closed her eyes. Her fingers tangled in my hair clenched and released, mirroring the pulsing waves of her pleasure.

Quickly I settled into a rhythm, judging the pressure of my tongue by the changing sounds of her breathing. My tongue danced lightly across her clit and then flicked within her. She stiffened for an instant and tried to thrust herself against me. I slid my tongue from inside her and sat back for a moment. A flush of color was spreading slowly across her chest. I went back to teasing her clit.

I was ravenous now, sensing that it required just a little longer for Christine to orgasm. My tongue thrumming across her clit was incessant. She drew in a sharp sudden breath and then began clutching at one of her breasts and plucking at the ruby red nub of her nipple, her head bowed over, watching me with wide mesmerized eyes.

When Christine came, it was with a growl in her throat and a convulsive bucking of her hips. My tongue stayed pressed to her pussy and the rush of her arousal was as warm and sweet as honey on my tongue.

Much later, when we were dressing, Christine told me she wouldn't be visiting any more. I never asked her why. Maybe she found a tree in a forest that had vines like long tentacles... or maybe she felt it was better to jump before she was pushed. We both knew right from the outset that our relationship was for the pursuit of a good time, not a long time.

Before we went our separate ways, Christine suggested offhandedly that I should write a book about some of the things I had discovered about women and sexuality.

So I did.

It was a novel about a fictional interview with a Master...

Which happens to lead me to my next question.

So what does reading erotica do for you? How does reading repay you in exchange for the time you give it?

Ever think about that?

I mean, reading erotica means something different to just about everyone. For many women, it's a chance just to deservedly unwind and relax for a couple of hours at the end of a frantic day after everyone in your family has made demands of your time. Reading is your little reward.

Or maybe you read erotica in order to live vicariously through the exploits of fictional characters. There's nothing wrong with that. Daily life is a grind and if your escape is into the fantasy of fictional erotica heroes, and that's how you take a rest from the worries of life, then who is anyone to judge?

Good for you.

Some ladies read because they are especially fascinated with an aspect of the erotica genre – most notable the BDSM lifestyle. For them, reading is a little like research, and they dream about maybe one day being able to experience for themselves some of the things their favorite characters experience.

How about you?

I write erotica books because it's a subject I know a little bit about. But I'm not the mystery here... you are!

I suspect your reasoning changes. I suspect you love books, love to escape into the pages of a compelling story... and the erotica genre allows you to enjoy harmless fantasies and at the same time maybe discover some fascinating stuff and sexy ideas along the way.

Am I wrong?

Tell me if I am. It's important because I want to understand you, and I want to know where you're coming from. That's what friends do, don't they. They listen and learn about each other.... just like we're doing, you and I, right now.

* * *

Do you like to watch?

It's a fantasy that a large number of women secretly think about; they dream about watching another couple having sex. Some submissive women crave the specific humiliation of watching *their* man with another woman...

Does this surprise you?

From personal experience I can tell you that having sex with another woman while your partner is watching is an enormous turn-on. At the dominant – submissive level, a Master might use such a scenario when training a slave.

How would you feel about watching your man or your Master pleasure another woman while you sat – only allowed to watch – on the edge of the bed, or maybe in a corner?

You see, submission comes in many forms; pain and specific humiliation are just a couple of aspects. I guess being a cuckquean falls into the latter category.

On two occasions I have brought another woman home for sex while the submissive sat and watched us. On one of those occasions the scenario blew up in my face – the submissive girl I was in a relationship with realized after the first few minutes that what she *thought* would be arousing was actually enraging…. so I won't talk about that night!

The other night though was a spectacular success and actually went on to become a semi-regular arrangement that worked well for all three of us; my submissive, the visiting woman and myself.

The submissive girl I was training was named Deanne. She was an athletic girl who was active in a number of sports. We had met at a local sporting event and over time began seeing each other exclusively for BDSM training sessions. Deanne was a willing student and a very obedient submissive. Everything she did was given the same careful attention and discipline as her sporting pursuits. She hated to lose, and she hated performing her submissive tasks to a less than excellent standard. At school she would have been the kid who always got gold stars.

Kimberly on the other hand was a different woman entirely. We had shared a few sexy weekends together before she had moved to a different part of the country a year earlier. She was a voracious insatiable fiend with long black hair and a willowy figure. She had a pretty face and a spectacular figure. I called her up and we talked. I mentioned my plan and offered to fly her in for a weekend.

Kimberly was on the next plane and Deanne was sitting in the back seat when we picked Kim up from the airport.

The two women were like fire and ice. Deanne was demure. She had a trim figure and brown hair. Her intensity was a total contrast to the wild-child personality of Kim.

When we arrived at my apartment, it was natural for Kim to hook her arm in mine, and we walked side-by-side to the front door with her hip and her breast brushing against my arm while Deanne followed, silent and pensive.

Kim was staring up into my face, smiling with big flirtatious eyes. When we got inside she threw her jacket over the sofa and stood with her hands on her hips, eye-to-eye with Deanne.

Kim made her intentions clear, taking the script we had roughed out over the phone and then ad-libbing outrageously. She told Deanne that I was hers to fuck for the weekend and that Deanne had better learn to love watching my cock in another woman's pussy. Then she told Deanne that she would sit and watch, but never comment, and never come. For the entire weekend she was to be denied the release of an orgasm.

Okay... well that hadn't gone quite to plan. I had intended an explanation that was more sensitive, more sensual. My style of domination was more sophisticated and reasoned. Kim's set of demands was like a slap in the face.

For long, long, *very long* seconds Deanne said nothing, but I could see the turmoil in her eyes – the simmering, lip-quivering outburst that hovered between her thin pressed lips.

Finally, to my bewildered surprise, Deanne nodded her head in capitulation and then lowered her eyes submissively to the floor. Kim shot me a glance over her shoulder and gave me a triumphant wink.

And I just about fainted.

Kim and I knew each other's bodies well, so there were no trembling moments of discovery or delight. We simply went into the bedroom and tumbled onto the mattress together like the long-lost lovers we were, and began kissing passionately. Out of the corner of my eye I could see Deanne standing in the threshold of the doorway with her arms folded across her chest. I felt Kim's hands rubbing across the hardness of my cock and then she fumbled with my belt buckle and zipper. I propped my head up on a mountain of pillows and ordered Deanne to strip naked. She did so mechanically, until she was ankle deep in her dress and underwear. I beckoned her to the edge of the mattress with a commanding gesture of my hand. She came on silent feet, her eyes fixed on mine, not daring to flick her gaze to where Kim was crouched on her hands and knees, freeing my hard cock from the restraint of my jeans.

I ordered Deanne to spread her legs. She fixed her gaze on a mark on the far wall, lifted her chin a little and shuffled her feet apart. Her hands went instinctively behind her and she pulled her shoulders back, presenting her pert breasts.

Her pussy was inexplicably wet. No, actually, not just wet. She was *really* drenched. My palm brushed across her clit and then I slid two fingers straight up inside her. Deanne gnawed on her lip and tried to stop her hips from bucking responsively.

Kim had my cock in her mouth, kneeling over me with her dress hiked up around her waist and her knees splayed wide apart. The buttons of her blouse had been undone and I could see the lace of her bra and the white mounds of her bulging breasts. I slid a hand up between her thighs and she stopped sucking my cock for just long enough to sigh encouragement.

My fingers found the dampness of her through the warm wet silk of her underwear. I glided my fingers back and forth, rucking the sheer fabric into the deep crease between her pussy lips, and Kim groaned again with a mixture of desire and anticipation.

At last she let my cock slide from between her lips and knelt upright on the bed. She was looking defiantly at Deanne as she slowly drew her panties down her thighs. She kicked the lace aside and quickly slipped out of her heels.

I laid Deanne on the bed, flat on her back and then Kim shuffled around until she was on her hands and knees directly above. The two women were looking into each other's eyes, Kim's breasts hanging out of her blouse. She spread her legs and I knelt behind her, swiping the swollen head of my cock slowly along her pussy until it was coated in her wetness. I pushed inside her gently, taking my time, and Kim's mouth hung open and her eyelids fluttered. Deanne was staring up, directly into Kim's eyes. She would have seen the look of rapture on Kim's face as my cock filled her – there was simply no way she couldn't have.

I began fucking Kim, using shallow teasing probes of my cock because I knew from experience that was what drove her into a sexual frenzy. My hands were on her hips. I held her under tight restraint to stop her pushing back against me, and as I slowly fucked her, my thoughts went to Deanne.

Was she insanely jealous, or maddeningly aroused?

I needed to know.

I pulled my cock from Kim's pussy and rolled her onto her side. I positioned myself behind her and Kim lifted one leg high into the air so I could enter her. This time I fucked her deeply with a hand wrapped around her waist, my fingers teasing her nipple while my cock plunged in and out.

Deanne was ordered to kneel over Kim's pussy and use her tongue to lick and please us. I told her she could masturbate but that she must stop before reaching orgasm. Deanne nodded dutifully and I let out a groan when I felt the flutter of her tongue as it swabbed enthusiastically between Kim's flared wet pussy lips and the base of my cock each time it disappeared deep inside Kim's sex. Deanne was fingering herself furiously. In less than thirty seconds she had to stop.

That was when I knew.

That was when I was sure cuckqueaning was going to work for us as a submissive training tool.

Deanne kept touching herself like she was stoking a fire, letting it burn down and then reigniting the flames by returning her hand to her pussy. All the while I continued to fuck Kim, urged on by her slutty vocal encouragement. When I came, it was deep inside her with Kim's own orgasm brought on by Deanne's tongue, licking contentedly at her clit while my cum trickled onto her tongue.

That weekend passed in a blur. Kim and I had sex half-a-dozen times: once in the back of the car while Deanne was in the front seat, naked and driving. Another time I made Deanne sit blindfolded beside the bed with her hands tied so that all she had was the sounds of us fucking, and her imagination. By the second evening Deanne at last gave up all pretense of merely being obedient and in a hushed, embarrassed rush of words she actually admitted that the weekend had been the most arousing experience of her life.

She had found her fantasy.

And so too had Kim.

Every woman has a fantasy…

* * *

Touch yourself!

Spread your legs right now and touch your clit. I want you to surrender to your arousal, forget your inhibitions, and just touch yourself.

Feel the tip of your finger slide just a small way inside your pussy – enough to provoke you – enough to make you throw back your head, and for your lips to part in a sexy little gasp. Can you sense your arousal? Can you feel the warmth spreading through your lower body; those first signs of sexual excitement? Can you feel yourself becoming wet and wanting?

Touch yourself!
Do it for you… and do it for me.

Don't make me come prowling out of the shadows. Don't make me kiss you because I honestly don't know where that will end. Right now everything that is instinctive to me is restrained on a tight leash. If I cross this room – if I get close to you… well I don't have the discipline to resist.

We've connected, you and I. We've become *intimate.*

So touch yourself. Let me watch you come. I want to see the look on your face at that exquisite moment of rapture. I want you to stare across the room right now and make eye contact with me as your breathing quickens and the beat of your heart begins to race.

Play with your pussy and imagine my hands running over your breasts, my kisses down your throat. Fill your mind with your own secret fantasies and give yourself over to the sound of my voice and your own sensual need. To be a good girl for me sometimes means you must be wickedly naughty. This is our moment.

Touch yourself!
I want to watch you come.

* * *

So where do we go from here, now that so much between us has changed in such a profound way?

We're different now, you and I. We have been made different by what we have just shared. It's enhanced the nature and intensity of our relationship.

By being so intimate.

I don't want to leave here and let the emotional connection between us just dwindle. I don't want this time to become just a fond reminiscence.

So can we meet again, sometime soon maybe?

I'll have more stories to entertain and arouse you. And you... well who will you be when we next meet? Will you be transformed in some way? Will you smile at me with a secret sense of anticipation when I arrive again?

I can hardly wait to find out.

Anticipation... *it really is everything!*

37174698R00037

Made in the USA
Lexington, KY
22 April 2019